MW00805129

Text copyright © 2004 by Kara LaReau
Illustrations copyright © 2004 by Jenna LaReau

All rights reserved. No part of this publication may be
reproduced or transmitted in any form or by any means,
electronic or mechanical, including photocopy, recording, or
any information storage and retrieval system, without permission
in writing from the publisher.

Requests for permission to make copies of any part of the work should
be mailed to the following address: Permissions Department, Harcourt, Inc.,
6277 Sea Harbor Drive, Orlando, Florida 32887-6777.

www.HarcourtBooks.com

Library of Congress Cataloging-in-Publication Data
LaReau, Kara.
Rocko and Spanky go to a party/Kara LaReau;
illustrated by Jenna LaReau.
p.   cm.
Summary: Sock monkeys Rocko and Spanky spend lots of time preparing to go to the birthday
party that they have been invited to attend.
[1. Monkeys—Fiction.   2. Toys—Fiction.   3. Parties—Fiction.   4. Birthdays—Fiction.]
I. LaReau, Jenna, ill.   II. Title.
PZ7.L32078Ro   2004
[E]—dc21   2003004988
ISBN 0-15-216624-6

First edition
H G F E D C B A

Printed in Singapore

Color separations by Bright Arts Ltd., Hong Kong
Printed and bound by Tien Wah Press, Singapore
This book was printed on 104 gsm Cougar Opaque Natural Woodfree paper.
Production supervision by Sandra Grebenar and Ginger Boyer
Designed by Jenna LaReau

ROCKO and SPANKY GO TO A PARTY

Written by **Kara LaReau**

Illustrated by **Jenna LaReau**

Harcourt, Inc.

Orlando Austin New York San Diego Toronto London

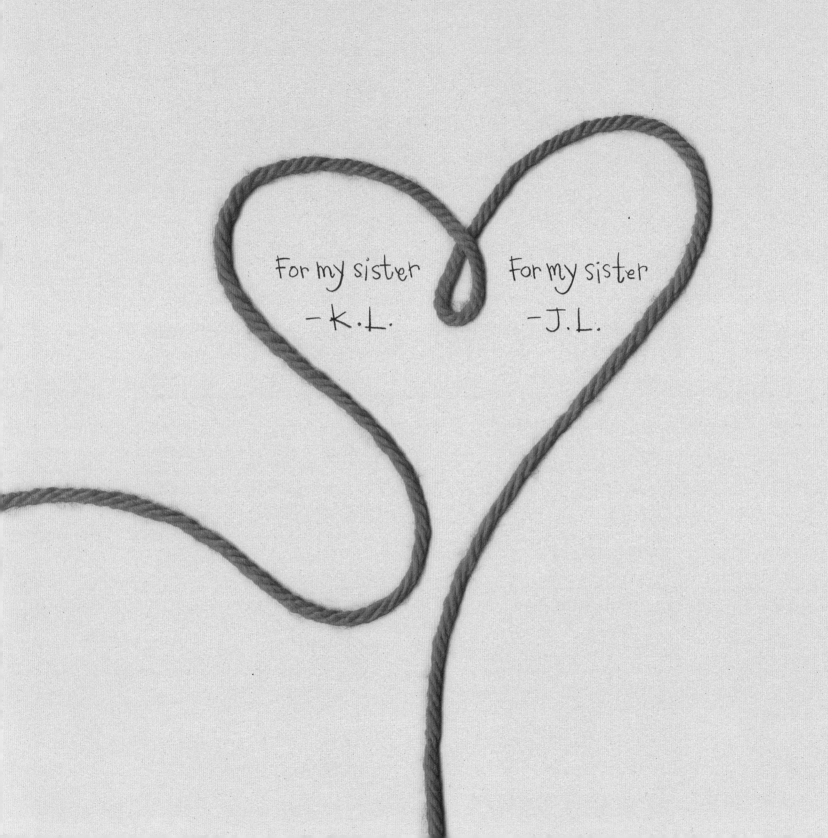

For my sister
  -K.L.

For my sister
  -J.L.

"Look! We're invited to a party at Shelly's," says Spanky.
"We'll need to bring a gift."

"Good idea," says Rocko.
"Let's motor."

"Check out all this great stuff," says Rocko.

"There sure is a lot to choose from," says Spanky.
"How will we ever find the right gift?"

"What about these skates?" asks Rocko.
"Everybody likes to **ROLLERBOOGIE!**"

"Not without safety gear,"
says Spanky. "Too dangerous."

"Then how about legwarmers?" asks Rocko.

"Um, those seem kind of . . . flashy," says Spanky.

"Look at these slippers," says Spanky. "SO glam."
"BO-RING," says Rocko.

"We need something fun," says Rocko.
"Like these maracas.

¡QUÉ BUENO!"

"Qué LOUD," says Spanky.
"At this rate, we'll *never* find a present."

Then, there it was . . . the perfect gift.

"Socks are so practical," says Spanky.

"Now let's get dressed," says Rocko. "What should I wear?"

"I know what I'm going to wear," says Spanky.
"I have my outfit all picked out."

"How do I look?" asks Spanky. "Isn't this vest *way* cool?"
"And WAY too big on you," says Rocko.

"What about these boots?" asks Spanky.
"Can I pull off the western look?"

"Please *do*," says Rocko.

"Then I'll accessorize," says Spanky, "with this elegant necklace."
"Hey, I just made that!" says Rocko. "The paint's not even dry."

Finally, Rocko and Spanky are ready.

"I'm so glad we helped each other," says Spanky.
"Me, too. I look GREAT," says Rocko.

"Time to go," says Spanky.

"Fasten your seat belt," says Rocko. "It's going to be a bumpy ride."

"Here's Shelly's house," says Spanky.
"But it seems awfully quiet."

SAND ST.

"Maybe no one is home," says Rocko. "Is today the wrong day?"

"It says today on the invitation," says Spanky.
"Let's ring the bell and see."

"How could you forget my birthday?" asks Rocko.

"How could *you* forget *my* birthday?" asks Spanky.

"We knew you wouldn't remember," says Shelly,
"so *we did*."

Rocko and Spanky are glad to have friends.
AND each other.

"What a perfect pair," says Rocko.
"And these socks are nice, too!" says Spanky.

HAPPY BIRTHDAY TO US!

The End

THANKS TO OUR FRIENDS

Allyn (our CHIEF), Scott P., Andrea, Michael,
Mom and Dad, Gram and Papa, Scott B., and Eden

This book was set exclusively with hip-happenin' fonts from House Industries (www.houseindustries.com).
Methods and materials used to create the artwork include: Photoshop; digital photography; acrylic paint; colored pencils; crayons; school glue;
construction paper; one pair of Red Heel socks; several handfuls of sequins, glitter, and chi-chi balls; two sets of maracas; gold stars; yarn;
rickrack; felt; and one large bag of assorted googly eyes.

ARTIST'S DISCLAIMER:
NO SOCKS, MONKEYS, OR SOCK MONKEYS WERE HARMED DURING THE MAKING OF THIS BOOK. HONEST.

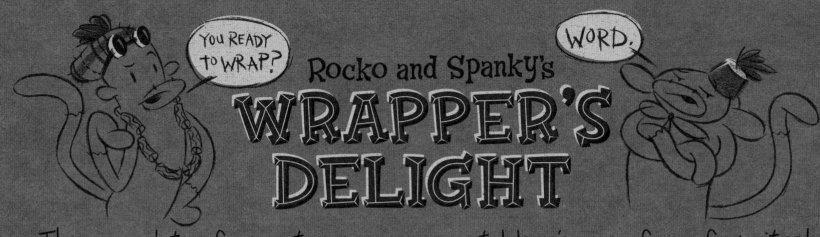

Rocko and Spanky's WRAPPER'S DELIGHT

There are lots of ways to wrap a present. Here's one of our favorites!

You'll need

- a paper bag (for a smaller gift, use a lunch bag; for a bigger gift, use a grocery bag)
- white school glue, scissors, and a hole punch
- colored tissue paper and construction paper
- about a foot of yarn (or ribbon)
- anything else you might use to decorate a gift (stickers, sequins, pom-poms, cutout shapes, and, of course, our favorite—googly eyes!)

STEP 1) Find a gift for that special someone.

STEP 2) Loosely wrap the tissue paper around the gift. Carefully place the gift into the bag.

STEP 3) Fold the top of the bag over to make a flap.

STEP 4) Cut a tag out of construction paper. Punch a hole in the tag, then address it.

HOLE MADE WITH HOLE PUNCH

TO: ROCKO
Love: Spanky

STEP 5) Punch two holes through the top of the bag. Thread the yarn through the holes and then through the hole in your tag. Tie the ends into a knot or bow. For added flair, cut fringe along the edge of the flap.

TO: ROCKO
Love: Spanky

TO: ROCKO
Love: Spanky

STEP 6) Now decorate. Be creative!

STEP 7) Present your *BEE-YOU-TEE-FUL* gift to your special someone.

And REMEMBER—

gifts are great for holidays, but they're best when people least expect them!